This book belongs to:

....

For Richard – J.K.
For Hannah – C.W.
For Archie – S.W.

OXFORD
UNIVERSITY PRESS
Great Clarendon Street, Oxford OX2 6DP

Oxford University Press is a department of the University of Oxford. It furthers the University's
objective of excellence in research, scholarship, and education by publishing worldwide in

Oxford New York
Auckland   Cape Town   Dar es Salaam   Hong Kong   Karachi   Kuala Lumpur   Madrid
Melbourne   Mexico City   Nairobi   New Delhi   Shanghai   Taipei   Toronto

With offices in
Argentina   Austria   Brazil   Chile   Czech Republic   France   Greece   Guatemala   Hungary   Italy   Japan
Poland   Portugal   Singapore   South Korea   Switzerland   Thailand   Turkey   Ukraine   Vietnam

Oxford is a registered trade mark of Oxford University Press
in the UK and in certain other countries

Text © Jane Kemp and Clare Walters 2006
Illustrations © Sam Williams 2006

The moral rights of the authors and artist have been asserted

Database right Oxford University Press (maker)

First published 2006

First published in paperback 2007

British Library Cataloguing in Publication Data available

ISBN: 978-0-19-272584-4

1 3 5 7 9 10 8 6 4 2

Printed in China

My First Toy Catalogue

Jane Kemp and Clare Walters

illustrated by Sam Williams

OXFORD

UNIVERSITY PRESS

Pigley and I love
to look at all the toys
in our big book.

soft, squishy baby bricks.

Smooth teddies, fuzzy teddies,

ready-for-a-cuddle teddies.

Long cars, racing cars,

slow and chunky wind-up cars.

Finish

Glove puppets, sock puppets,

dancing-on-a-string puppets.

Rag dolls, princess dolls,

walking, talking baby dolls.

Fire trucks, dumper trucks,

digging-up-the-ground trucks.

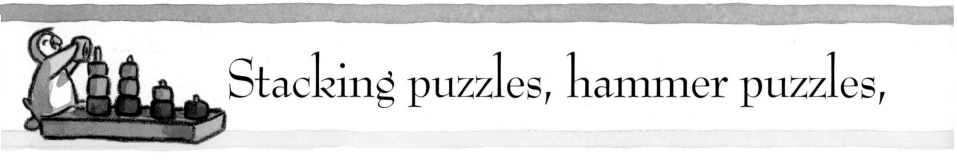

Stacking puzzles, hammer puzzles,

fit-together picture puzzles.

Big trains, little trains,

puffing-there-and-back trains.

Farm animals, wild animals,

floating-in-the-bath animals.

So many toys
and all such fun,

but, Pigley, you're
my number one!

From babyhood onwards, you and your child will have lots of fun simply pointing at and talking about all the toys in this book. As your child starts recognising objects, shapes, colours, and numbers, you'll find this book a perfect resource for encouraging that development. Here are just some ideas for you and your child to enjoy together.

1. There are four elephants in this book. Here are three.

Can you find the other one?

2. Can you find

a green cross?   a blue star?   a red heart?

3. Can you find five crowns?

4. Two of the toys in this book have a little wind-up key. Here is one. The other wind-up toy is an animal. Can you find it?

5. Can you find three flags?

6. Can you find these little ducks in a row?

How many are there? Can you quack like a duck?

7. Who is wearing

a green collar?   a red head-scarf?   a spotty bow-tie?

8. Can you find this train puzzle?
How many blue wheels does the train have?

9. Can you find this stripy rabbit and can you spot what has been taken away in this picture?

10. Do you know these colours and shapes?

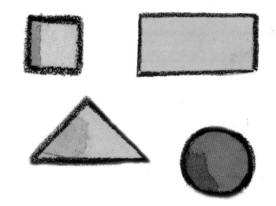

6. The three little yellow ducks are on page 25.   7. The dog on page 25 is wearing the green collar, the pirate doll on page 17 is wearing the red head-scarf, the yellow teddy on page 11 is wearing the spotty bow-tie.
8. The train puzzle is on page 21 and it has nine blue wheels.   9. The stripy rabbit is on page 24 and he is missing his carrot.   10. Blue square, yellow rectangle, green triangle, red circle.